No, No, Gnome!

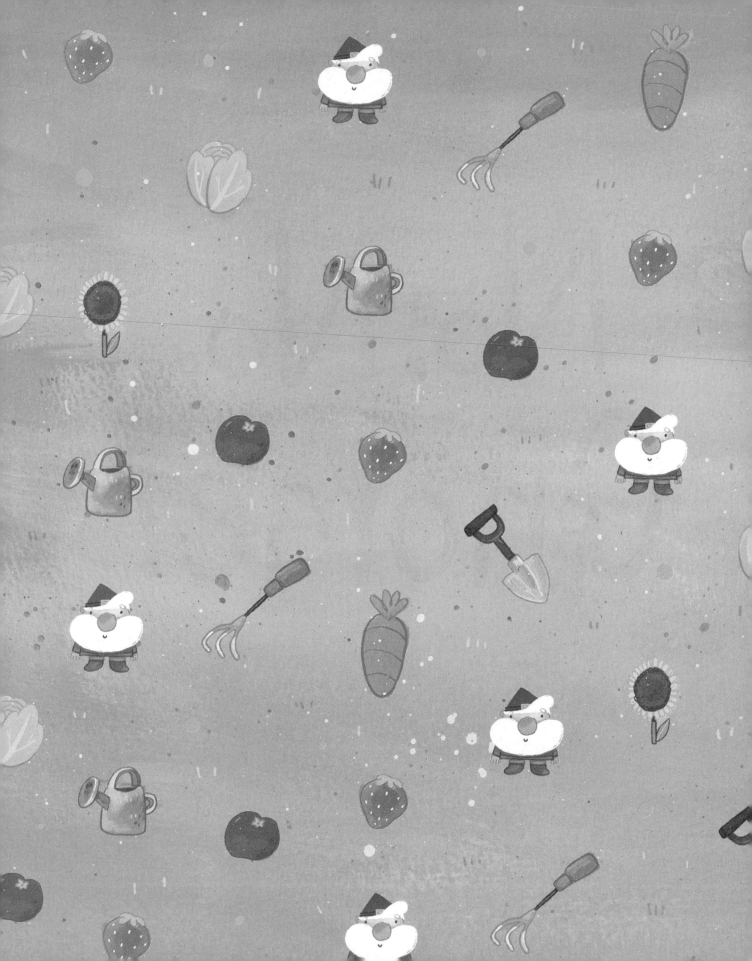

For Gavin, the teacher

ISBN 978-1-338-18718-2

12 11 10 9 8 7 6 5 4 3 2 1   17 18 19 20 21 22

Printed in the U.S.A.   40

First Scholastic printing, March 2017

Book design by Chloë Foglia
The text for this book is set in Barcelona.
The illustrations for this book are rendered using a combination of gouache and Photoshop.

No, No, Gnome!

ashlyn anstee

SCHOLASTIC INC.

The students at Greenthumb Elementary had been working hard on their garden all year long.

Finally it was almost ready to harvest!
Everyone was excited.

Especially Gnome.

As the students headed outside, Mr. Waters assigned each of them a task.

The kids quickly got to work.

At first, Gnome was helpful.

But then . . .

Mr. Waters suggested
Gnome try something else.

But pretty soon . . .

Mr. Waters gave Gnome
one last chance.

All Gnome had to do was stand still and hold the basket for the garden clippings.

But Gnome didn't even last one minute.

Mr. Waters sent Gnome
back to the classroom.

When the other kids returned,
no one said hello.

At recess, no one
would play with him.

And at the end of the day,
no one said good-bye.

Gnome
was
blue.

How could he show his friends
that he was sorry?

The next day, Gnome couldn't wait to get back to the garden.

The other kids were dreading it.

But when they went outside . . .

The students got to work
picking their harvest bounty.
Gnome was helpful.

Most of the time.

Ashlyn Anstee grew up in a rainy city, traveled to a snowy city, and then settled in a sunny city, where she works as a story artist for animation. She has two thumbs, and neither of them are green. Her first book was *Are We There, Yeti?*, which she wrote and illustrated.